Hocus and Pocus

and the Dragon Next Door

HOCUS AND POCUS
and the Dragon Next Door

A. R. Capetta

illustrated by Charlene Chua

CANDLEWICK PRESS

This is a work of fiction. Names, characters, places, and incidents are either products of the author's imagination or, if real, are used fictitiously.

Text copyright © 2025 by A. R. Capetta
Illustrations copyright © 2025 by Charlene Chua

All rights reserved. No part of this book may be reproduced, transmitted, or stored in an information retrieval system in any form or by any means, graphic, electronic, or mechanical, including photocopying, taping, and recording, without prior written permission from the publisher.

First edition 2025

Library of Congress Control Number: 2024944214
ISBN 978-1-5362-2493-1 (hardcover)
ISBN 978-1-5362-4269-0 (paperback)

24 25 26 27 28 29 LEO 10 9 8 7 6 5 4 3 2 1

Printed in Heshan, Guangdong, China

This book was typeset in ITC Mendoza.
The illustrations were created digitally.

Candlewick Press
99 Dover Street
Somerville, Massachusetts 02144

www.candlewick.com

EU Authorized Representative: HackettFlynn Ltd.,
36 Cloch Choirneal, Balrothery, Co. Dublin, K32 C942, Ireland.
EU@walkerpublishinggroup.com

For Sammy, Emily, Walter, and Malcolm
ARC

For Home At Last Rescue—
thanks for helping Catsby
CC

FOLKS OF INKWELL

Highly Magical Pet
HOCUS — she / her

Highly Magical Pet
POCUS — he / him

Witch
JINX — she / her

Witch
ARCHER — he / him

Wizard
OFELIA — she / her

Warlock
TAM — they / them

Chapter One

The Potion Drop

Hocus and Pocus lived in a big purple house filled with magic and mischief. They knew every perfect napping spot. They knew where Jinx, their witch, stored treats for them—and for the apprentices who came to study magic each day. They knew which shelves the spell books went on.

They knew every tree in the yard and toadstool in the garden.

"Now that you know the house so well," Jinx announced one day, "it's time to learn about your neighborhood."

"How do we do that?" Hocus asked, her ears perked with interest.

"I have an idea," Jinx said.

"Potion drop?" Archer asked.

"Oh, I love potion drop day," said Tam.

"Po-tion drop!" chanted Ofelia. "Po-tion drop!"

"Hocus, I know a lot about potions now," Pocus said. "But why would you want to drop one?"

"Hmmm," Hocus grumbled. "I don't know." She used her special magic to look into Jinx's eyes and see what would be happening in exactly two minutes—but it wasn't anything about potions. It was just lunch. "I guess we'll have to wait."

The next day, everyone took a walk. "The town of Inkwell is not very large," Jinx said. "And this street, which loops around in a circle, is our neighborhood."

Jinx led them to the door of each brightly colored house. She gave potions to the people who lived in each one. "Isn't

this great?" Archer asked. "It's like reverse trick-or-treating."

They gave out all sorts of spells—for stopping runny noses, growing bigger roses, and helping people stay calm in a pinch. There was even a potion that let someone change into another animal for the day. One of their neighbors wanted to be an earthworm. "So grounding!" Jinx said. "Now you'll know the joy of having five hearts."

In return, people gave Jinx all sorts of things. Nonmagical neighbors traded pickled vegetables and fresh-baked lemon pies, knitted socks and stacks of firewood.

A witch who made potions, like Jinx, gave them a spell for finding lost spells. Warlocks had nature magic—their warlock neighbor gave them a nice day in a jar. Wizards were good at using enchanted objects, and enchanting them, too. A very kind wizard saw the puppies and ran off to get an enormous bag of magical flavor-change chew sticks.

"I love potion drop day," Hocus said, a treat hanging out of her mouth. It changed from peanut butter to turkey as she trotted to the next house.

Pocus trailed behind, trying not to panic. Some of these bushes smelled funny. There were wild animals around. The squirrels looked like they might secretly be attack squirrels.

By the time they looped around to the last house, Pocus was ready to hide under a pile of soft hats and pretend none of this had ever happened.

Then the last neighbor opened the door.

"That's Jade, and his pronouns are he and him," Ofelia whispered. "He's our next-door wizard."

"Oh, hi there, Jinx, Archer, Ofelia, Tam, pups. You might want to back up. I have a new pet, and I'm having some trouble getting her to . . . stop setting things on fire."

"Jinx taught us ten magical ways to put out a blaze," Ofelia said. "We're not afraid of fire."

"I am very afraid of fire," Pocus said. No one noticed, though. Jinx and Tam could only speak a little bit of puppy, and the rest of the humans didn't know how.

Hocus was busy leaping like a pogo stick to get a look at the new pet.

"We'd love to meet her," Jinx said. "When she's ready."

"Just . . . don't eat the neighbors, okay, Bye-Bye?" Jade pulled the door open all the way. Right there, guarding the house, glaring out at them, unfolding actual wings . . .

was a dragon.

"This is the best news of the best day," Hocus said. "We can be best friends with the dragon who lives next door!"

Pocus had already run halfway home.

Chapter Two
A Not-Scary Spell

"Pocus, why don't you want to be friends with Bye-Bye?"

"I have friends," Pocus said. "You, Jinx, Archer, Ofelia, and Tam. Five friends is a lot."

Hocus loved making new friends. Her idea of a lot wasn't five—it was more like five hundred. But she was different from her brother. She would have to find some way to talk him into it. "Dragons are highly magical pets, like we are. Bye-Bye can fly without a broom! Bye-Bye can breathe fire! Haven't you ever wanted to breathe fire?"

"No . . . Have you?"

"Of course!"

Pocus poked his nose out of the hat pile. "Jade said Bye-Bye might crisp us and eat us, and I think that is a good reason *not* to be friends."

"Fine," Hocus said. "But you can't get scared and run away every time you see the dragon next door."

"Why not?" Pocus asked.

"There might be something *even scarier* that you run into because you are running away from Bye-Bye."

Pocus didn't like that answer.

Hocus had known he wouldn't.

"I will have to brew a not-scary spell," Pocus said. "And I can take it whenever

I go for a walk." Pocus felt like that would solve a lot of his problems. Bye-Bye wasn't the only thing he'd thought was scary on their walk, after all. Just thinking about the squirrels, who were probably attack squirrels, made him shiver.

"I don't think Jinx has a not-scary spell," Hocus pointed out.

"You just said that we're highly magical pets. I can make up a spell of my own," Pocus said.

"Hmmm." If she could get Pocus to be less scared of the dragon, maybe they could get back to her plan of all becoming best friends. A spell was worth a try. "What goes in a not-scary spell?"

"Things that don't make me scared, of course."

Hocus and Pocus both ran around the house, gathering the things Pocus was least afraid of: Jinx's wool socks, a spell book written in green ink that he liked to nibble just one corner of, and a piece of bat jerky.

"Now we need a cauldron," Pocus said.

But the ones in Jinx's potion room were full. And she'd put the rest of them away when she was puppy-proofing the house. So they licked Pocus's dinner bowl clean enough that they could brew the spell in it.

They nudged and nosed in the socks, the spell book, and the jerky.

"What's next?" Hocus asked.

Pocus tried to think of what Jinx did when making her potions. Sometimes she said special words to them! "We need an incantation. Say the least scary words you can think of."

"A roll in the mud," Hocus chanted. "Zoomies around the garden. Chicken dropped on the floor!"

"Lap naps," Pocus added. "So many lap naps."

"Everything is just sitting in the bowl," Hocus said. "What turns it into a potion?"

"I think . . . these things are supposed to melt?" Pocus said.

"If only one of us could *breathe fire* like a certain *dragon* I know of," Hocus said. "Wait! Potions are liquid! There's no liquid in there. We have to add some."

"I'm not afraid of our water bowl," Pocus said, and then added, "anymore." He *had* been a little scared of it when Jinx first put a self-filling spell on the bowl.

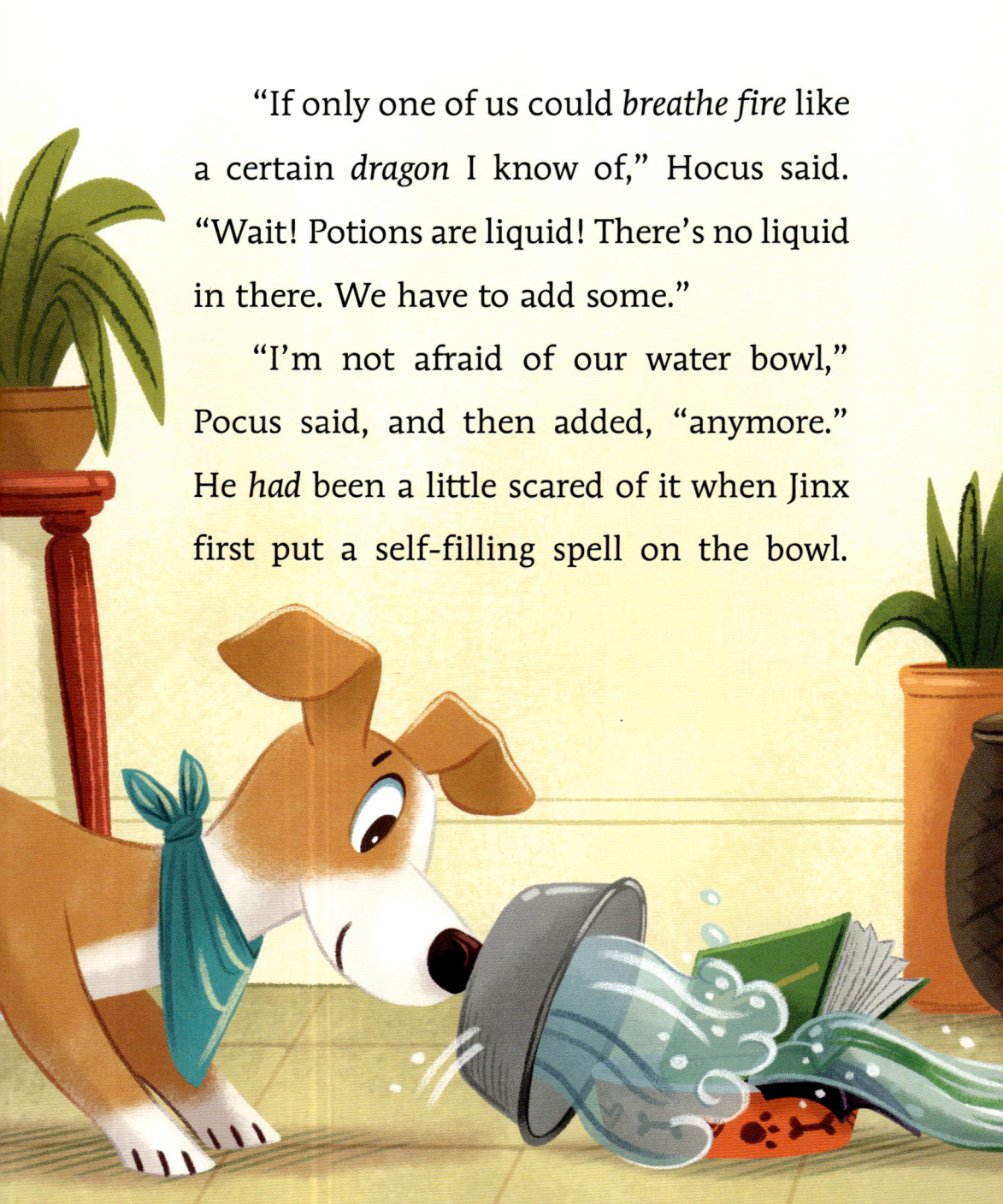

It gurgled when it filled back up. Gurgling could be scary.

Hocus nudged the water bowl and tipped it over. The food bowl flooded. The bat jerky turned soggy. The socks started to float. The green ink from the spell book ran and the whole thing turned into a weird green mess.

"Hey, it looks like a potion now!" Hocus said.

"We forgot to get a potion bottle!" Pocus cried.

Pocus lapped some up straight from the floor. Maybe it would work without the bottle. Maybe he wouldn't be scared of Bye-Bye—or the rest of his neighborhood—with a green tongue and a belly full of magic.

Hocus lapped up some of the potion, too. You could never be too not-scared—right?

Chapter Three

Wrong

Hocus bounded toward Jade's yard. Feeling the boldest she had ever felt—which was pretty bold—she bounced up and hooked her paws on top of the gate.

"Hocus, what are you doing?" Pocus asked.

"I'm going to visit Bye-Bye!" Hocus said, using her brother as a stool. With his help, she sailed right over the gate. "Come on, before the potion wears off and you get scared again!"

Pocus did feel strangely brave. Maybe the potion *was* working. Still, "I can't get there *now*," Pocus said. "There's no one left for me to stand on."

Hocus was too distracted to feel bad about that detail. "This yard is *amazing*."

Then something caught Hocus's eye. "Um, there is a cave and Bye-Bye is in it and she does *not* look happy to see me," Hocus said.

"You are supposed to be invited *before* you leap into someone's house. Or yard. Or face."

"What do I do now?" Hocus asked.

Pocus thought hard. "Say, 'Is it okay that I'm here right now? If not, I can come back another day.'"

"Is it okay if we play right now and I come back every day?" Hocus asked.

"That's not what I said!" Pocus yipped.

Hocus was feeling too not-scared to notice the difference.

"Hi, Bye-Bye!" she said with a big playful pounce toward the cave.

Bye-bye puffed a bit of smoke.

"I won't touch your treasure, if that's what you're worried about," Hocus said. "I feel that way about the stuffed octopus Archer gave me."

Bye-Bye snuffled fire.

"Fantastic!" Hocus shouted. "Can you teach me to breathe fire? Can we play hoard-and-seek?"

Hocus crept a little closer. But it seemed Bye-Bye didn't want her that close to the cave—she rushed out, chasing Hocus toward the treasure pile.

"This isn't working, Pocus!" Hocus shouted. "Please help!"

Pocus ran into the house to look for a human.

Once Hocus was on top of the tiny mountain, Bye-Bye stopped chasing. But Hocus was stranded. And she was pretty sure by now that Bye-Bye didn't speak puppy.

How was she supposed to fix this and become best friends with Bye-Bye?

When she looked down into Bye-Bye's big, purple eyes, Hocus's magic showed her what would happen in exactly two minutes.

Hocus wouldn't be in Jade's yard anymore. Bye-Bye would be back in her cave, shivering with fear.

"Are . . . you afraid of dogs?"

Bye-Bye whimpered. It reminded Hocus of the time Pocus thought the water bowl was a gurgling monster.

"We were wrong!" Hocus shouted. "Bye-Bye isn't scary. She's *scared*."

Pocus wasn't there to hear the news.

Hocus wanted to tell Bye-Bye that she wasn't a dangerous dog. She was a delightful dog. A daring dog. A dog who would make a very good friend for a nervous dragon.

"I wish you *did* speak puppy," Hocus said. Wait—maybe she had it backward. Maybe *she* could speak *dragon*.

If she could just get to Jinx's potion drop bag.

Chapter Four

Fire & Fang

Pocus skidded to a stop in front of the gate, with the apprentices right behind him.

"Pocus, what's going on?" Ofelia asked.

"Why did you drag us out here?" Archer asked.

From the other side of the fence, Bye-Bye roared.

"Dragon!" Tam said. "Pocus needs help and it has something to do with the dragon."

"What?" Archer asked.

"That's what Pocus was trying to tell us inside the house," Tam said. "I didn't catch all of it." Tam was a plant and animal warlock, and speaking with creatures was part of their magic. "I keep meaning to learn more puppy, but I get distracted! There are so many exciting languages, like squid and squirrel and dragon and . . ."

The apprentices looked at the gate again. They couldn't see the dragon, but they could see Hocus.

Archer rushed to unlatch the gate.

Bye-Bye fled back to her cave, and Hocus shot back into Jinx's yard.

"How did you get over there?" Tam asked.

"Mischief gymnastics," Hocus said. "And some help from a not-scary spell."

"You're alive!" Pocus shouted.

"Of course." Hocus rushed past her brother and sped inside.

A minute later, a dragon trotted out of the big purple house.

"Ahhh!" Pocus cried.

"It's me," Hocus grumbled, but in dragon, it came out as *RRHGGH!* and a little puff of smoke.

Pocus decided it was his job to protect the apprentices from this strange dragon. So he put out one! terrifying! fang!

"Oh, put that fang away," Hocus said. "You can't tell it's me? I used Jinx's potion that changes you into another animal for the day."

"Leave! Now!" Pocus jumped and yipped.

"Pocus . . ." Hocus sighed. It came out as a stream of fire.

"Ahhh!"

Hocus didn't have time to explain. And even if she did, Pocus didn't speak dragon.

It was time to get back to Bye-Bye. Hocus spread her new wings. They weren't as big as she thought they would be. And they weren't very strong. But they were strong enough that she could flap over her brother's head and into the yard next door.

"Now there are *two dragons?*" Pocus cried. There were not enough soft hats in the world to make him feel less worried.

Chapter Five
The Most Worried Bubble

An hour later, the apprentices were packing up to go home. "It's getting late," Archer said. "Where's Hocus?"

"I don't know," Pocus said. "I've been busy hiding under the table and worrying."

They checked Hocus's favorite spots in the house. Pocus even went and peeked over the gate into Bye-Bye's yard. Just in case.

Hocus wasn't there.

Pocus had never lost his sister before. This was a new kind of scary.

"Oh, bats," Jinx said. "We should go out into the neighborhood and look for her before it gets too dark."

"I can't," Pocus said in a tiny voice. "There are dragons out there."

"What if I taught you some dragon words?" Tam asked. "If you and the dragons can understand each other a little better, you might be less scared."

"Maybe," Pocus said.

Tam taught Pocus how to say *hello* in dragon. They also taught Pocus to say *yes, no, thank you, goodbye,* and *please do not fry my toes.*

"You could wear my enchanted fire shield," Ofelia offered.

"That would help," Pocus said.

"Let's bring my broom," Archer suggested. "I can fly you right back home if anything gets *too* scary."

"Yes, please," Pocus said.

Jinx, Pocus, and the apprentices spilled out of the purple house and into the street. They called out, "Hocus! Hocus!" and someone ran over right away. But it wasn't Hocus.

It was Jade, the next-door wizard.

"Hocus is missing?" Jade asked. "Bye-Bye is missing, too!"

Pocus could see that Jade was upset. He rubbed his head against Jade's leg.

Pocus's special magic took the wizard's bad feeling and turned it into a giant purple bubble.

Pocus ate it with a snap.

It was the most worried bubble he had ever tasted. And he was someone who knew the many flavors of worry.

"We'll help you look for Bye-Bye," Pocus said. "And we won't stop until we find them both." Yes, he was still afraid of dragons—but Jade was even more afraid of losing Bye-Bye.

Pocus needed all his bravery to search the neighborhood at night. As the sky grew dark, the moon and stars came out. So did most of the neighbors. "How can we help?" they asked.

"Hocus and Bye-Bye are both missing," Jinx said.

The apprentices looked high. The neighbors looked low. Jinx and Pocus looked everywhere between.

Jade was fretting. "What if Bye-Bye ran away?" he asked.

"I feel certain that she'll turn up any minute," Jinx said.

The good news was that Bye-Bye turned up right *that* minute. The bad news? The other dragon was chasing her. They both flew low to the ground in a wild zigzag. The second dragon spewed flames, lighting half the neighborhood bushes on fire.

Jinx and the apprentices ran around, using the ten enchanted ways to stop a blaze.

Jade shouted, "Bye-Bye! Bye-Bye, come back!"

Pocus wanted to find Hocus and go home.

But the not-scary potion was still in his stomach, and Pocus wasn't going to let anyone hurt his next-door-dragon.

Besides, that other dragon looked *truly* ferocious.

"I'm coming, Bye-Bye!" Pocus yelped.

Chapter Six
Hello, Bye-Bye

Pocus caught up right as the dragons stopped on Jinx's front lawn. He rushed toward Bye-Bye. "Hello!" Pocus said in dragon. It came out with a cough, since he couldn't puff smoke.

Bye-Bye screeched and flew straight up.

She landed on the top branch of the tallest tree in Jinx's yard.

Jade rushed over. "Oh no, oh no," he said. "Now she can't get down."

"But she has wings," Ofelia said.

"Young dragons don't fly very high," Tam explained. They knew lots of good

dragon facts. "Most are scared of heights, and their wings are still growing. They get stronger and braver as they get older. That is probably the highest Bye-Bye has ever been."

"Because *someone* scared her," Hocus said in puppy. She still knew how to speak puppy of course—she just had to work hard to switch.

"Did you say something?" Pocus asked.

"Yes," Hocus said. "I'm your sister."

"That's impossible. You're a terrifying dragon!"

The dragon opened her mouth. Pocus cowered, waiting for the roar of flame.

But there was no fire. The dragon was just sticking out their tongue. And it was *green*.

A very magical shade of green.

"Hocus?"

Hocus sighed a big, fiery sigh. Pocus almost got roasted by it, even with Ofelia's enchanted fire shield.

"*You're* the ferocious dragon?" Pocus asked.

"You really think I look ferocious?" Hocus said happily.

"We have to get Bye-Bye out of that tree!" Jade said. "But my enchanted ladder is broken."

"Brooms should do the trick," Jinx said.

Archer and Jinx flew up to where Bye-Bye was perched. But Bye-Bye was still scared, and she wasn't budging.

"I have an idea!" Pocus ran back inside. He brought out a dog bowl with just a few drops of green potion left in it. "Hocus, can you fly this up? It will help Bye-Bye be not-scared enough to fly down!"

Hocus flew to the top of the tree, carrying the dog bowl. And Pocus. She landed with a little crash.

"That was a lot of work," Hocus said. "My wings are tired."

"Hello, Bye-Bye," Pocus said in dragon.

"We're here to help," Hocus said, also in dragon.

"Why did you bring a dog?" Bye-Bye asked.

"Oh, that's just Pocus," Hocus said. "*He* came up with a plan to get you down. All you have to do is lick this bowl."

"How do you feel now?" Hocus asked. "Less scared?"

Bye-Bye shrugged. "I feel the same."

"Nothing happened!" Hocus told Pocus. Well, not nothing. Bye-Bye's tongue *was* bright green.

"The not-scary spell didn't work?" Pocus asked. "You mean . . . I've been brave all day *without a spell?*"

Every fear that Pocus hadn't felt all day rushed in at once. It was like getting hit with a fireball. Getting hit with a fireball while sitting on a small branch at the top of a very tall tree.

And now squirrels were climbing up the trunk.

"I've been learning squirrel," Tam shouted helpfully. "They're saying, 'Our tree! Our tree!'"

The squirrels started throwing acorns at Hocus, Pocus, and Bye-Bye.

"I knew they were attack squirrels!" Pocus said. "Hocus, you will have to fly me and Bye-Bye back down," he added in a whisper.

"I can't," Hocus whispered back. "The not-scary spell didn't work. Remember? And young dragons are afraid of heights. Which means *I* am afraid of them, too."

Which meant all three of them were stuck in a tree with the attack squirrels headed their way.

Chapter Seven
What Else Can a Dragon Do?

The squirrels had climbed to the second-highest branch.

"Bye-Bye, please fry their toes," Pocus said, putting together the words Tam had taught him in dragon.

"No," Bye-Bye said. "They think I'm bad already."

"But you haven't *done* anything bad," Hocus said.

"It doesn't matter." Bye-Bye cried a few crystal dragon tears. "They don't want me in their tree. Nobody wants me. As soon as we get down, I am leaving."

"But we just became friends!" Hocus cried. "And everyone down below the tree wants to help you. Even Pocus is helping, and he was scared of you at first!"

Pocus barked at the squirrels. He looked very concerned that they were about to climb the last few branches and reach him.

"He's scared of everything at first," Hocus admitted.

"I'm scared my wizard isn't happy," Bye-Bye said. "I keep him up all night with my snuffle snore. I scorched his favorite couch."

"Pocus and I were the same kind of scared when Jinx brought us home from the shelter for slightly magical pets. But we felt a little better every day. And you will, too." Hocus wanted to help her new friend feel the way she did now. Like she had a family, a home, a neighborhood.

But the squirrels were really not helping.

"Are you sure you don't want to toast them and eat them for an after-dinner snack?" Hocus asked.

"I missed my dinner, and I am very hungry, but I don't eat squirrels," Bye-Bye said. "I eat hot coals."

"You *do?*" Hocus asked.

"Why do you think I burp fire when I'm nervous?"

"Those are your *burps?*" Hocus asked.

"Do you want to see what else I can do?" Bye-Bye asked.

"Yes!"

Bye-Bye breathed fire—it looked like fire—but it was bright blue instead of

orangey red. When it hit the squirrels, it didn't burn them. It made them turn blue and stop climbing.

Pocus poked at a nearby squirrel with one paw. It didn't move.

"What is that?" Hocus asked, amazed.

"Freeze breath," Bye-Bye said. "They'll be unfrozen in a minute or two. Some dragons have magical breath powers. But when I'm scared, only fire burps come out."

"We helped you be less scared?" Hocus asked.

"I think so," Bye-Bye said.

"Enough to fly back down?" Hocus asked.

"I think so!" Bye-Bye spread her wings and glided down from the tree. The landing was clunky, but she didn't seem to mind.

Jade ran forward and scooped her up in both arms. "Oh, my little dragon. Let's get you home."

"Thank you, friends," Bye-Bye called back.

"Bye-bye, Bye-Bye!" Pocus called. "Now, how do *we* get down?"

The apprentices already had that part figured out. They'd been busy running all over the neighborhood gathering one important item from every house.

Now they placed them all together beneath the tree.

"Soft hats!" Tam shouted. They pointed to a pile the size of a small mountain. "Your favorite."

Chapter Eight
Highly Magical Friends

The next time Jinx did a potion drop, Pocus stayed home. He liked his neighbors, but seeing every one of them in a single afternoon was a little too much.

Jinx had a new helper, though.

When they got home, everyone gathered in the potion room.

"Pocus, I've been working on something for you," Jinx said.

Pocus spun around in circles, excited for the gift.

"When I cleaned up the spell book and the bat jerky and my socks and your food bowl, I could see that you were trying to brew your own potion. So I had a little talk with Hocus. She called it your 'not-scary spell.' It was impressive for a first try," Jinx said. "You'll get it next time. For now . . ." She reached into her potion drop bag and pulled out one last bottle.

"This is for you. It's *not* a not-scary spell. It's natural to be scared sometimes. And never feeling scared can get you into a special kind of trouble."

"Maybe," Hocus grumbled. "Sometimes."

"This is my 'stay calm in a pinch' spell. A bit of this every day will keep you calm enough to remember that you are already very brave. A not-brave dog would never have gone up a tree to save a dragon."

Pocus lapped up the potion. It even *tasted* calm.

"Hocus, I have something for you, too," Jinx said. "Fire burp sauce! It's pretty much just hot sauce, which is not the same as breathing fire, but—"

Hocus leaped with joy. "I love it."

"It's time for our playdate with Bye-Bye," Ofelia said. "Everybody ready?"

"Are you playing dragon tag again?" Pocus asked. That was the game Hocus and Bye-Bye invented the night they both disappeared. It involved flying very fast and not getting tagged by a flame.

Pocus found it terrifying. Even *after* the stay-calm spell.

"No," Hocus said. "We're going to play hoard-and-seek. Jinx said we could use the fun stuff people gave us for potion drop day as the treasure."

"Oh!" Pocus said. "I do like hoard-and-seek."

"Do you want to play? There would be . . . seven friends."

"Seven friends doesn't sound *too* scary," Pocus said.

"This is going to be perfect!" Hocus said. "Well, it would be a little more perfect if we had wings." And she looked straight into Jinx's eyes.

"Did you say *wings?*" Jinx asked.

She grabbed a cauldron.

Exactly Two Minutes Later

It was the best game of hoard-and-seek the neighborhood had ever seen.

The squirrels were not invited.

DON'T MISS!

HOCUS AND POCUS
and the Snow Day Sorcery

Look for the next book in the series,
coming in 2026!